ALMOST BROTHERS

Edna Walker Chandler

Illustrations by Fred Irvin

Albert Whitman & Company • Chicago

In addition to aid given by many librarians, particularly those at the University of Arizona, Tucson, I wish to acknowledge the generous help of Julio Escabedo, Consultant in Intergroup Relations, Department of Education, Sacramento, California, for information on Mexican-American culture; Robert Watson Kaniatobe of the Choctaw Tribe, student in Anthropology and Native Arts, San Francisco State College, for research aid on the Yaqui Indians; and Karen Thule, for assistance in supplying source material.

EDNA WALKER CHANDLER

Cover Photograph: Bob Glaze. ARTSTREET. Chicago

ISBN 0-8075-0289-8   Library of Congress Card 77-165817
© 1971 by Albert Whitman & Company, Chicago
Published simultaneously in Canada by George J. McLeod, Limited, Toronto

CONTENTS

1 Left Alone

Benjie Brave pulled the pillow over his head. He wanted to shut out the morning light. This was a bad day. He knew it.

Today Benjie's big brother Charley was leaving for college. Jean, his sister, had already gone to boarding school. She was sixteen. Only Benjie would be left at home.

A scratch and a thump under the bed made Benjie reach down to pet old Nosey. That dog knew something was wrong, too.

For the thousandth time, Benjie wished the Braves were still in South Dakota. Up until a few weeks ago that had been the only home Benjie knew. His father, Dr. Brave, had worked at the Indian reservation hospital, and his mother had been one of the nurses.

Benjie could speak in Sioux as well as in English. He liked the snowy winters, the little town, and horseback riding. The boys there were his friends. Here he felt lonely and homesick.

"Why did my dad come to Arizona?" Benjie asked himself. "Sure, he can be head of the hospital here. But this is an awful place! It's a desert. Nothing grows here but a lot of prickly cactus. It's hot and I hate it. And now I'm going to be all alone after Charley goes."

Nosey whined as if he knew Benjie's thoughts. He wanted to remind the boy that he, Nosey, wasn't going anywhere.

Just then Charley himself pulled the pillow off Benjie's head and called, "Up, up! My bus leaves for Tucson at noon. I've got a few things I want you to keep while I'm gone, Benjie."

Benjie guessed Charley was trying to make the good-bye time easier. But he couldn't help saying, "Charley, don't go! You don't need more book stuff and college. Stay here in Manzanita with us."

"Doing what?" Charley asked.

"I'll bet you can be a tourist guide or work at the cement plant or something."

That made Charley laugh. He was stubborn about ideas, just like Dr. Brave. "Benjie," he said, "I know what I want to do, and you know it, too."

"Yeah, be a big-shot lawyer so you can help Indians get their land back. It won't work."

Charley gave his little brother a push and said, "That's how you think now. Just wait. You'll change your mind."

Benjie knew Charley was set on doing what he planned. At the moment he almost hated Charley for being so stubborn. But that feeling didn't last.

"OK," Benjie said. "Where's the stuff you want me to keep for you?"

"Here," Charley said, pulling a box out from under his bed.

Benjie jerked the lid flaps open. Inside were Charley's treasures. There was his old softball which had been through a lot of games but was good for more. Also there was the trophy football with the names of Charley's teammates written on it. In the bottom lay a faded, worn sweatshirt.

"Sure, I'll take care of the stuff for you," Benjie said, holding the football carefully.

"Use the softball all you want, but I'd kind of like the football kept for me. OK?"

"Sure. Guess I'll go out and play around with the softball."

Benjie pulled on his clothes while Charley looked at the mess on his own bed. His suitcase was half packed and a box partly filled.

Benjie scooped up the ball and started for the door. Nosey followed him.

"Don't forget to come back," Charley called. "That bus just might be on time."

Charley went to the window and tried to see the desert through his brother's eyes. It was pretty bare. South Dakota even in summer had been a lot greener than this.

Charley remembered back to the time when the Braves had moved from California to the

Dakota reservation. That was before there had been any little brother.

It had been hard for Charley to find new friends, but he had made it. He had learned to be proud of his Indian family, for the Braves were Sioux and Arapahoe.

From the window, Charley could see most of the little town whose Spanish name, Manzanita, means "little apple." It was really just a bus stop with one store and a gas station. The school where Benjie would go sat on top of a mesa nearby.

A couple of cottonwood trees grew near the village well. People visited there when they came to get water. Indians and Mexicans came in old cars and trucks. They unloaded empty oil drums, filled them with water, and hauled them home.

Water was a problem in Manzanita. Charley hadn't been here long, but he knew water, enough of it, could make a big difference.

Beyond the school, Charley could just see the hospital. It had its own wells and pumps to supply water. Dr. Brave was proud of the new hospital—but it was already too small.

Far in the distance, smoke from the cement plant darkened the sky. It used much of the water the people could have used in their homes. But many Indians and Chicanos—the Mexican Americans—wanted the plant. It was their only way to earn money for things they could not get from the desert.

Some people got government help, but it was very little. They needed the jobs at the cement plant, they needed water, too. So what could the people do?

Charley turned back from the window to his packing. Maybe he could find the answers in college, some of them at least.

Time flew. Soon Charley heard his mother call, "It's nearly eleven o'clock. Is Benjie with you?"

"He's out playing with my old softball," Charley answered. "I don't think he's far." He could hear his mother calling "Benjie!" as he took his things out to the car.

Benjie came up from a little gulley back of the house. He was dirty and he looked unhappy.

"Benjie Brave, you're a mess!" his mother exclaimed. "Get in the house and clean up. I'll help you because it's late."

Soon there were loud cries from the bathroom. "Ouch! That's my ear. Mother, you'll rub my face off!"

When Benjie and his mother came out, his face was shining like a new copper penny. But it was not a smiling face.

In the car on the way to the bus stop, Benjie made one last try to keep Charley at home.

"Charley, don't go. We can be winter tourist guides. Lots of people come here in the winter. I heard that in the store. Lots of visitors come to see the Indian celebrations. We can learn about the celebrations and you won't need any more book stuff for that."

Charley laughed. "That's where you're wrong. A guide has to know a lot besides the trail he's following. But I'm not going to college to learn to be a tour guide, even if it is fun."

Benjie sighed and gave up. Charley was stubborn, just plain stubborn.

At the bus stop there was a feeling in the air

that something was about to happen. The people waiting together often looked north, toward Eloy.

Benjie had this something-about-to-happen feeling, too, but he didn't like it. He knew what was going to happen. In a few minutes a big bus would rush down toward everyone waiting. It would stop, grab up everyone with a suitcase or a box, and off it would go. And Benjie would be left behind without a big brother.

It was hard enough when Charley had gone away while the family lived in South Dakota. But at least he had come home on weekends. Here, he could only come home for holidays.

There was a sudden move in the crowd, then a shout. "It's coming! The bus is coming!"

Young people who were going away took firm hold of suitcases, boxes, and packages. Last-minute good-byes filled the air.

To Benjie, everything was a jumble of sound. He couldn't understand much of what was being said. It was a mix-up of Indian and Spanish words and a little English. It was just too much!

12

A handsome, dark brown man turned to Benjie's father and in a pleasant voice asked, "You are Dr. Brave?"

Holding out his hand for a friendly handshake, Benjie's father answered, "I'm Dr. Brave, and this is my family, except our daughter, Jean. She's already away at school. And you are—?"

"Juan Mendoza. This is my little son, Juanito."

A boy about Benjie's age grinned shyly but said nothing.

"My older son goes to college today. For his second year," Mr. Mendoza went on.

"And our older son, Charley, is going, too," Dr. Brave said. Looking at Benjie's cloudy face, he added, "We'll miss him. But we know our children will be doing what they should."

What they should! Not the way Benjie saw it. There were so many more interesting things to do than go to school.

While the bus stopped and the driver got out to check tickets and load luggage, Dr. Brave and Mr. Mendoza talked.

"We are glad to have the hospital and a doctor," Mr. Mendoza said. "Before you came, a doctor had to come from Tucson. He did not stay here. Now we have a doctor who lives among us. This is good."

"Thank you," Dr. Brave answered. "We hope we can make the hospital a good place where sick people can get well. We want a clinic, too, where people can learn how to stay well."

"You will be busy," Mr. Mendoza said. "People will come from all the little villages around here when they know we have a good doctor."

"That's what we want," Dr. Brave said.

"You may be so busy you will need a bigger hospital. Then I can help. I am a builder. My friend Tony Garcia is a good builder, too. He works at the cement plant part of the time. I am doing some building there, too."

"I'll remember you, Mr. Mendoza," Dr. Brave promised.

By now the bus tickets had been checked, and the passengers were going up the steps.

"Well, I guess this is about it," Charley said. He rumpled Benjie's thick black hair. "Take

15

care of Mom and Dad, kid. Don't let them work too hard at that hospital. And Nosey, here, keep that hound dog out of trouble, too. OK?"

Benjie mumbled something like "I will." He wasn't going to make a fuss, anyway not here. Out of the corner of his eye he could see Juanito Mendoza watching. Who does he think he is, anyway? Benjie wondered and swallowed hard.

Dr. Brave was saying, "We're behind you, Charley. You'll do all right." He gave his tall son a slap on the shoulder and a quick handshake.

Charley leaned down to kiss his mother good-bye. He only looked at Benjie and stuck out his hand.

Benjie took that strong brown hand and would not let go—not until the bus driver said, "All aboard for Tucson!"

Charley was the last one up the steps. That left Benjie standing close to the bus. Much too close. His mother pulled him back.

"Benjie!" she said. "You'll get yourself run over. It isn't the end of the world. Charley will be home for Thanksgiving."

Without answering his mother, Benjie jerked away. Thanksgiving was too far away even to think about.

So what does a guy do when he feels bad and he has no friends and he's a stranger? A mist came over Benjie's eyes. He felt Nosey's slick wet tongue licking his hand.

Benjie watched the big bus as it began its trip to Tucson. He watched until it disappeared down the highway.

Benjie turned toward a little path leading off toward the mesquite-covered hills. Nosey followed him.

Mrs. Brave called, but Benjie kept on going. He had to get away from the bus stop and all the people. He didn't want Juanito with his round face and big curious eyes staring at him.

Benjie Brave ran on along the path, kicking the sand into dusty whirls as he went.

2 Feeling Strange

The bus taking Charley away had gone through Manzanita on Saturday. On Sunday, the Braves went to the little adobe church near the school.

After church, people came up to speak to Dr. Brave and his family. Mr. Mendoza came over to introduce Tony Garcia while Mrs. Brave and Mrs. Mendoza visited.

Some of the boys shoved each other around to get Benjie's attention. He pretended he didn't see, but he couldn't miss the round face of Juanito Mendoza. He looked friendly today, not just curious.

18

As everyone walked toward the cars, Juanito said something Benjie didn't understand. Benjie looked at him and shook his head.

"You speak Spanish?" Juanito asked.

Again Benjie shook his head.

"You are Indian—you speak Navajo?"

Benjie began to feel stupid, and it wasn't a good feeling. "I speak Sioux. Can you talk Sioux?" he asked, sure Juanito would have to say no.

Dr. Brave spoke then and said, "Benjie, you need to learn Spanish. Our whole family does. People here all know English and Spanish, and some speak Indian languages, too."

"He will learn Spanish at school," Mrs. Mendoza said. "The other children are good teachers."

The very sound of that word school made Benjie's stomach begin to turn over.

A school had taken his brother far away. A school nearby was about to take the last of his own freedom.

"See you mañana," Juanito called as he turned toward the Mendoza car.

"Mañana, that means tomorrow," Mrs. Brave said with a laugh. "I know that much."

At home, Benjie changed his clothes and ate lunch. Then he was ready to enjoy what was left of the day. He took Charley's old softball and went outside. Nosey ran after him.

"If Charley were here, we'd have a game of catch," Benjie told Nosey. "And if I just had a brother my age, he wouldn't go away and leave me."

Nosey trotted along, his sharp foxlike nose smelling whatever excitement might be around. Benjie rubbed the dog's ears and said, "Well, old boy, you're one friend I can count on. I don't have to learn some new talk to make you understand."

Mrs. Brave had warned when Benjie set out, "Don't go too far. Dinner will be ready about five o'clock."

"OK, I'll be careful," Benjie had promised. He'd already decided to explore Brush Canyon, and that should give him enough time.

Now as he walked along the trail leading into the canyon, Benjie saw berries still on the manzanita shrubs. He knew you could eat those berries and make a drink from the juice.

But these berries were dry and had very little taste. He spit them out. He was so sure that he was all alone that he jumped when a voice said, "Manzanita is not good now—too late."

Benjie looked around, and Nosey barked sharply. The voice sounded close, but no one seemed to be anywhere in sight.

"You don't see me? Look again!"

That voice—Benjie was sure he knew it. But it was Nosey who found the speaker. Juanito was crouching against a big rock in the path. Benjie could almost have stepped on him.

Juanito laughed. "No desert eyes," he said. "I could hear you coming. I went to my friend's house, but I guess they went to a fiesta somewhere. Nobody home."

Juanito looked curiously at Benjie, but he waited for Benjie to say what he was doing out here in Brush Canyon.

"I'm not going anywhere," Benjie said. "Nosey—that's my dog—and I are just sort of exploring."

"Come and I will show you something good to eat—better than manzanita," Juanito offered.

Benjie followed the Chicano boy down a rocky cliff. There were piles of red rock in the desert here. They looked as if a big shovel had spilled a load of red rock and sand.

Juanito found a cactus with a thick, fat leaf. He split a leaf with his knife and peeled off the prickly skin. Then he cut a piece of the cactus and gave Benjie a bite.

The cactus had a sweet taste, almost too sweet.

"Candy cactus," Juanito explained. "Some people make real candy from it and sell it."

"It's sweet all right," Benjie said. "Play catch?" He showed Juanito the softball.

"OK," Juanito answered.

It wasn't much of a game. The boys tossed the ball back and forth, but they often missed. Nosey had a good time chasing the ball. Sometimes he had to do some hunting to find it.

For a while the game went better, then Benjie called, "Catch this!" and threw the ball as hard and far as he could toward Juanito. He reached high, but missed it.

Both boys went over the rocks and into the chapparal looking for the ball. Even Nosey couldn't find it.

Suddenly the old dog began to bark in an excited way. He was on the other side of a big rock and the boys ran to him.

"Where's the ball?" Benjie asked, then he saw a boy playing catch all by himself.

"Hey, that's my ball!" Benjie shouted.

Juanito yelled, "Tomasito!" and something in Spanish Benjie couldn't understand. He was sure it meant the ball was to be given back.

The boy turned and threw the ball toward

Benjie. Then Benjie had an idea.

"Let's play three-corner catch," he said, throwing the ball to Juanito, who called to the new boy.

Juanito threw the ball. The boy missed, Juanito spoke in Spanish and pointed at Benjie to show the boy was to throw the ball to him.

The ball came spinning toward Benjie, and he missed. Benjie threw to Juanito, and he missed!

When Benjie looked for the new boy, he was gone. He'd hardly turned his back, and Tomasito had disappeared just like that.

"Where did he go?" Benjie asked. "Doesn't he want to play?"

"He went home," Juanito said, not seeming to care one way or the other. "The Yaqui kids don't play with us much even at school."

"Yaqui kids?" Benjie repeated. "Who are they?"

"Indians," the Chicano boy said. "They live in a little village of their own. I see this kid at school. But most of the Yaqui kids don't come much. They stay home or go away to work. I don't know." He shrugged.

24

Benjie thought he knew a lot about Indians, but Yaqui was a new name to him. He had never heard of these Indians who had come from Mexico years ago. The Yaquis keep to themselves and like their own ways.

"Tell me the boy's name again," Benjie said.

"The teachers call him Thomas, but we call him Tomasito. I don't know his Yaqui name."

"Let's go to his village," Benjie suggested. "I'll bet it isn't far."

Benjie looked around as he spoke. He had already explored all of Manzanita too many times. Maybe this would be something new and interesting to do.

"Better not. Yaquis don't like strangers much —except when they have a fiesta. A public one, I mean. Then everybody gets friendly and happy."

"How soon?" Benjie asked. A fiesta sounded like a little excitement.

"Oh, Yaquis have small fiesta days," Juanito said, looking uninterested. "But the big one is at Easter time. Everybody gets friendly and happy then and everybody goes. I mean *every-*

25

body." And now Juanito grinned, thinking of good times.

"Easter!" Benjie said, disappointed. "That's a long time off. Way after Christmas."

"Si," Juanito agreed, and reached into a pocket of his jacket and brought out a small paper-wrapped package. A tamale.

Suddenly Benjie noticed that the shadows were getting long. The late afternoon sun was putting a glow on the red rocks and on the sand of the desert. It must be almost dinnertime at home. His stomach was growling.

"Say, I've got to get home," Benjie said to the Chicano boy. "See you mañana. Come, Nosey."

"Adios. See you mañana," Juanito called and bit into his tamale.

Benjie said the words over and over all the way home.

Adios, mañana, adios, mañana. What a good sound they had. Maybe he could learn to speak Spanish. Then he could talk to everyone, Mexicans, the other Indians, even the Yaquis. He wondered if he'd see Tomasito tomorrow—mañana.

26

3 An Invitation

Benjie walked to school alone the first day. He had no big brother to tag along with, no friendly dog to keep him company.

Only children in the first six grades went to Manzanita. Older kids took a bus to Casa Grande.

Benjie had seen some of the children at the store, but they acted as if they had never seen him before. Juanito Mendoza was the only one who looked friendly. Tomasito, the Yaqui boy, stayed with other boys who looked like him.

Maybe the Yaqui village was close enough so all the boys walked over together, Benjie thought.

"Hola," Benjie said, trying to say hello in Spanish. But Tomasito did not answer and only talked to his friends. Benjie could not understand the words, but he understood the looks. These boys were sorry for him, a boy who couldn't talk to anyone.

"What's the matter with them?" Benjie asked Juanito. "Are they laughing at me?"

"A little," Juanito admitted. "It is the way you talk. You are an outside Indian."

Feeling angry inside, Benjie turned away from the Yaqui boys. The Chicano boys were different. They knew Juanito and Benjie were already friends.

There were other Indian girls and boys at school, too, Apache, Pima, Navajo, and Papago. Benjie liked the sound of those Indian names and when no one was listening, he said them to himself—Apache, Pima, Navajo, Papago.

The language business was really hard for Benjie. Everyone rattled off Spanish talk a mile a minute. He was dazed and left out of everything. The Yaquis were the worst. They kept to themselves and even at lunchtime ate in a little group of their own.

The school itself was all right as schools go. The three teachers were friendly and tried to make Benjie feel welcome. They spoke English and Spanish and used both in teaching.

At last the first long school day was over. Benjie didn't feel like going straight home because his mother was still working at the hospital.

"Wait for me," he called and ran after Juanito. The two boys went down the hill to the store.

"Big day," Juanito said, pointing toward all the people around the store and in it.

There were more people than Benjie had seen on other weekdays. Old cars, trucks, and horses were parked or tied near the store. The crowd was all Indian and Chicano, no tourists at all.

Benjie had learned long ago while he was in Sioux country that tourists almost always came in new cars or campers, that they carried a lot of cameras, and went around snapping pictures and asking questions.

"What's going on?" Benjie asked. "Why's everyone here?"

"It's check time," Juanito answered. "Most of the people got some kind of government help check last Saturday. Today they come to spend it for beans, canned meat, things like that."

Just then Juanito and Benjie saw Tony Garcia. He smiled at the boys and called out "Hola!"

With Tony was an old Indian man. His thin gray hair was long and tied with a red string. He wore an old T-shirt and brown pants much too big for him.

"Hola," answered Juanito. "Hola, Grandpa Jim."

Juanito spoke in fast Spanish, and Benjie could not understand even one word. But Juanito explained to Benjie in English.

"Grandpa Jim is very old. He is a Yaqui. He came from Mexico long ago. He doesn't even remember when. Every month he gets old-age government money."

Benjie nodded. He understood about that. Even if there were jobs enough at the cement

plant, Grandpa Jim was too old to work.

Juanito went on, "Tony brings him in to get his groceries. If Tony can't bring him, someone else does. Everybody kind of looks after Grandpa Jim."

"That's good," Benjie said.

"People like to see Grandpa Jim dance in the fiestas, especially the Pascua celebration at Easter. Only last year he didn't dance very long. I guess he got tired. Wait till you see him —Grandpa Jim is a maestro."

"What's that?" Benjie asked.

Juanito was quiet for what seemed a long time. Then he said, "I can't tell you."

"Is it a secret?" Benjie asked, curiosity beginning to eat him.

"No," Juanito said slowly. "It isn't a secret. Everyone goes to see the Yaqui Pascua celebration. It is just that it is kind of mixed up. Too hard to tell you."

Hearing that, Benjie made up his mind he was going to see the Easter celebration. But that was months away. He wanted something to do now.

Tony called Juanito and the two talked, in Spanish, of course. Twice Benjie heard his own name. He was sure they were talking about him and he began to feel angry. "I'll go home," he thought, and he turned to go away.

Juanito called him. "Come back, Benjie. Tony asked if you can come to his farm with me. I help him clean out his stable sometimes. Then he lets me ride his pony or the donkey. It is fun."

Benjie's angry feeling melted fast.

Juanito said, "Tony's farm is near. He'll take Grandpa Jim and the groceries to the Yaqui village and then come home."

"I'll have to ask my mother," Benjie said eagerly. "I can phone her at the hospital. Maybe the storeman will let me use his phone. Can we go with Tony to Grandpa Jim's?" This seemed a wonderful chance to see that Yaqui village.

"No," Juanito said. "You are an outside Indian. Anyway, I don't think Tony wants to take us."

"Juanito is right," Tony said in English. "Someday, but not now. You go and ask your mother if you can go to my house. If she says yes, start walking with Juanito."

"OK," Benjie said and pretended he didn't care about not seeing Grandpa Jim's home. Just the same, he was going to do that sooner than Juanito or Tony thought. When Benjie wanted to go somewhere or do something he was just as stubborn as his big brother Charley.

Inside the store, Pablo Chavez let Benjie use the phone, but he wasn't to talk long. The store was a busy place with people buying lots of different things.

Mrs. Brave said Benjie could go. She was glad to have him making friends.

"Be sure to start home early enough to get here before dark," she told him. "We don't want to send a search party out after you."

Benjie laughed, "I won't get lost, Mom. Don't worry. Nothing exciting like that will happen to me. I promise. And besides, Juanito has to be home when his father gets back from the cement plant."

Benjie had no idea he was making a promise he might not be able to keep.

4 One Stubborn Donkey

A rabbit jumped out from behind a barrel cactus and took off as Benjie and Juanito came close. They were on their way to Tony Garcia's.

"Look at him go!" Benjie said. "Too bad Nosey isn't here."

"You can get water from a big old cactus like that," Juanito told Benjie.

"Let's try it," Benjie said.

But Juanito shook his head. "Look at that thing! It is big and full of thorns. I heard Indians used to make fish hooks from thorns like that. You have to chop the top off the cactus to get the water. I don't think it tastes very good anyway."

35

"So what good is it?" Benjie demanded.

"Well," Juanito said, "sometimes people are pretty glad to have water from a barrel cactus. Like Tony once. He knows the desert and doesn't take any chances. But once he drove out looking for some lost sheep. He got caught in a sandstorm. His car got stuck in the sand. The motor was too hot to run. He poured all the water he had into the car. It ran a little way and stopped again. There was Tony—no car, no water. He saw a barrel cactus and he knew he had water to drink and waited for help to come."

Benjie thought about that. He could see that it was important to learn how to live in this desert country. That wasn't something he was going to learn in school. Juanito and Tony, and maybe even that Yaqui Indian boy Tomasito, could teach him a lot.

"I'll tell my big brother Charley about that barrel cactus when he comes home from Tucson," Benjie said.

"See those hills?" Juanito asked, and pointed toward the east. Benjie nodded.

"A lot of piñon pines grow there. Piñon nuts are good. In October we go to get them. You can go with me if you want."

"Sure, I'd like to go," Benjie answered. "I like piñon nuts we buy at the store. It would be fun to find them for myself."

The boys walked along without talking. The sun, even though it was late afternoon, still felt quite warm. Benjie wished he could go barefoot as Juanito did. But his parents seemed to think there was some kind of magic in a pair of shoes.

"Is it far to Tony's place?" Benjie asked.

"Not much farther. Lots of time to get there, stay a while, and get back before dark," the Chicano boy answered.

"Anything special there?"

"Oh, I don't know. Tony's house—casa, we say, his kids. They're little. I told you about his trail pony and donkey. Come on, I'll race you! Then we can have time to ride."

The boys ran fast. Juanito was soon ahead. He had no shoes to hold him back, and he knew every foot of the rutted old road. He stopped and waited for Benjie to catch up.

"Mira, look!" Juanito said and pointed. "Casa de los Garcia."

There was an adobe block house with a fence around it made of tall ocotilla planted close together. No one could climb a thorny fence like that.

Four small children played in the yard. Their mother, a pretty young woman, came out of the house as the boys turned into the yard.

"Hola," Juanito greeted her.

"Hola, amigos," she answered smiling. "You come to clean the stable?"

"Si, Senora Garcia," Juanito answered. "My friend Benjie wants to help. Tony said he could. He will be home soon. He went to take Grandpa Jim home."

"I know," said Tony's wife. "You go on to the stable. You know what to do."

"Si, si, Senora Garcia. Tony will find us."

As the boys walked toward the stable, Benjie asked, "Why does Tony keep horses? He has a car to go places."

"He likes horses," Juanito answered. "If you look for gold mines, a horse is good to have."

For a second, Benjie thought Juanito was trying to fool him. But the boy looked serious.

"Mines? You mean people still look for gold mines around here?" Benjie asked, stopping in his tracks. Maybe this wasn't such a dull place after all.

Juanito laughed now. "Sure! There are lots of gold mines around here. I don't know if anyone finds gold, but I know one thing. Everybody thinks he is going to."

"You mean Tony? How about you?" Benjie asked. "Wouldn't you like to find gold? Just ask me—I would!"

This time Juanito shrugged his shoulders. "Sure, I'd like to find gold. But did you ever hear about those old Spaniards who hunted for the Seven Cities of Gold? A long time ago . . ."

Benjie said nothing. He was thinking. He had a faraway feeling he had read something like that in a schoolbook, but it hadn't seemed important.

"I think it was all a bunch of lies," Juanito said. "I guess some people think Coronado found those cities. But he got sick and died and everyone with him died. Other people think he died looking for gold. Come on, I'd rather ride than talk about gold."

"I'd sure like to see what a gold mine is like," Benjie insisted. "Have you ever been in one?"

Juanito only said, "Mines are black inside. The walls can fall in."

"Well, I suppose an old mine could be dangerous," Benjie admitted. "Still I'd like to explore one."

"Maybe someday," Juanito said. "We have to work now."

When the boys reached the adobe stable, there were no animals anywhere. Juanito found the fork and wheelbarrow for cleaning.

"You can push the wheelbarrow along," he said. "I'll use the fork. Then we'll take that old broom and sweep out the stalls. Tony takes good care of his animals."

"What does he call them?"

"The pony's name is Marco Polo because he likes to go far places. The donkey is called Lightning, but not because he's fast. He's tricky."

40

"I bet I can ride them both," Benjie said. "I rode a lot where we used to live."

From outside the stable came the rattle and sputter-pop of a car being driven in. The pony and donkey heard the noise and came running from the nearby gully.

"It's Tony," Juanito said. "Let's hurry."

Tony stopped to see his family. The boys could hear the children laughing and saying, "Hola, Papa, hola! Did you bring us something?"

Just as the boys finished and were putting the tools away, Tony came to the stable. He saw they had done their work well.

"Gracias, amigos," he said. "Maybe I can do something for you someday. For now, here's this." And he tossed a candy bar to each boy.

"How about letting us ride?" Juanito asked.

"OK, but watch the sun. It's getting late. Juanito, you take Marco Polo. Benjie here can take Lightning. If he falls, he won't have so far to the ground."

"I won't fall off," Benjie declared, half angry. "I rode horses lots of times in South Dakota."

"Well, Lightning gets ideas," Tony said. "He's too lazy to run. I keep him because he's a good pack animal. But riding a donkey isn't like riding a horse. He might surprise you."

"Where are the saddles?" Benjie asked.

"Oh, you don't need saddles for a little ride. Just a bridle. Juanito can help you."

"I can put the bridle on Lightning," Benjie said.

The boys were soon mounted. The sun was already low in the sky and the shadows were long.

"Keep together," Tony warned. "Benjie could get on the wrong trail easy."

Both boys nodded, and Juanito gave the pony a slap with the reins and was off.

Benjie followed on Lightning. He liked the easy, side-to-side motion of the donkey's body. But he wished the animal would kick up a little dust.

The boys rode along, calling back and forth.

The desert air was cool now. It was full of pleasant clean smells Benjie liked but couldn't name. The rocks and tall saguaro cactus made shadows on the sand.

42

"See that hill ahead?" Juanito called. "When we get there, we'll turn and go back. This pony is spoiling for a run. I'll give him the reins and let him go. I'll wait for you at the hill. OK?"

"Sure!" Benjie yelled. To himself he said, "Next time I'll ride the pony. I wish this donkey would *move*."

Juanito and Marco Polo were soon far ahead. Then suddenly Lightning surprised Benjie by turning off on a little trail leading down into a gully.

Benjie pulled hard on the reins, but the donkey would not obey. He had his own ideas about where to go.

Nothing Benjie could do helped. Lightning made his way down into the gully, walking faster as he did so.

Benjie shouted and pulled on the reins. "Whoa! I'll walk back, that's what!" he said. But the donkey paid no attention.

Before Benjie could slip off, if he had really meant to, Lightning had another surprise ready. At the bottom of the gully was an old stream bed, flat and nearly smooth. Lightning

44

began to run—he ran as if something had bitten his heels.

Benjie forgot all about slipping off. Anyway it was impossible to do now. He could only hope the donkey would soon tire.

All at once, the donkey stopped without any warning at all. He raised his hind legs and rump. Off Benjie went, over Lightning's head and onto sandy earth.

A soft blanket of darkness came down over Benjie's head. He lay still.

5 Trouble!

When Benjie came out of the darkness and sat up, the donkey was gone. Benjie rubbed his head. He found a big bump, and it hurt.

"Juanito! Juanito!" he called as loudly as he could, but there was no answer. Maybe Juanito had already passed by the gully, calling but getting no reply. By now, he might be far away, still looking for Benjie without success.

Benjie moved his arms, then his legs. Everything worked.

The sun was almost down, but he could see the sandy riverbed. The first thing he had to do was get up out of this gully. Now which side had that crazy donkey come down? The boy hadn't the least idea.

Benjie tried to climb up the steep banks at different places. He always seemed to come to something he could not get around or through or over—huge rocks or clumps of cactus too prickly to get through. And although he stopped to listen for anyone calling him, he heard nothing.

"Well," Benjie thought, "I guess I'll be sleeping here if no one finds me soon." That was a scary idea, and Benjie called again and again. But only the cry of some kind of bird answered him.

The sun had set by now. Benjie's teeth began to chatter. He was afraid, deep down scared. He had to try once more to find a trail out of the gully.

He walked along the riverbed, looking and looking. Suddenly he saw horse's hoofprints. Or were they made by a donkey? It was so dark he couldn't be sure. There seemed to be a trail leading up a steep bank. He started to climb it.

As he felt his way up the path, he told himself, "I don't think I came down this way. I think it was the other side. But this is a trail, and it must lead someplace." And someplace—anyplace was better than spending the night in that dry riverbed. Nobody would find him down there.

Around the rocks the little path went, up the bank, through manzanita, between cactus clumps, and finally out into a clearing.

Just ahead was a cluster of small houses. Benjie's first thought was that it might be Manzanita, but nothing looked familiar. Too many houses for a farm like Tony Garcia's, he thought quickly. Maybe this was one of the little Indian villages he'd heard about but never seen.

There were lights in some of the little houses, as if the people had just lighted kerosene lamps. Benjie thought of lights burning at home, of his mother wondering where he was. Had Juanito or Tony Garcia told her he was lost?

There was something strange about this village. Some of the houses had a big wooden cross in the yard. Benjie had never seen anything like this. Did he dare go to a door and ask for help?

Before Benjie could decide what to do, a dog barked. Then another and another. People opened their doors to see what was happening.

Benjie tried to be as brave as his name. He stood as tall as he could and walked toward the house with the biggest cross. People of all sizes stood in front of the house.

Benjie tried to tell what had happened. But no one seemed to understand. He tried speaking very slowly. "I—am—lost. I went—for—a ride. The donkey—ran—away."

People began to talk to each other, but no one spoke to Benjie. It was an Indian language. Benjie could not understand a word. What would these strange Indians do to him?

A boy came into the yard where all the talking was going on. Benjie stared in surprise —he knew this boy. It was Tomasito! Then this must be the Yaqui village. And as if to prove his idea, Grandpa Jim, the old man Tony Garcia had brought to the store, also came outside to talk.

Children and grownups, old people and young, were closing in around Benjie. Some looked friendly, a few did not.

It was really dark by now, and Benjie knew he couldn't find the trail out of the village, even if he knew which direction to go. Which he didn't. Should he use Tomasito's name and speak to him? He wasn't sure. What about Grandpa Jim?

While he was wondering what to do, Tomasito said something to the tall dark man who had first seen Benjie. The tall man said something to Grandpa Jim, who nodded.

Tomasito looked toward Benjie.

Benjie wanted to say, "You have to believe me! I got lost. I came here by accident. I didn't come to spy on you. Please help me." But he just stood silently and waited.

Grandpa Jim went back into the house, but came out again with a flashlight. He gave it to Tomasito, who flicked the switch. Flashing the beam around the circle of people, Tomasito let it stop on Benjie.

"Come," he said. Was Tomasito really going to help Benjie? The boy couldn't be sure, but he had no choice but to follow.

Tomasito, guiding with his flashlight beam, led Benjie to the edge of the village yards, out toward a still unseen road. From then on, it was easy walking.

The deep darkness pulled away as the moon came up. Sometimes it was so light that Tomasito turned the flashlight beam off. There were long shadows in the moonlight made by the desert plants.

Benjie tried to talk to the Yaqui boy, but with little success.

Benjie felt sure Tomasito understood some English. He listened to the teachers and did what they asked him to do at the school. But he seemed not to want to talk to Benjie, an outside Indian.

On and on the two boys walked. Maybe it really wasn't as far as it seemed to Benjie, who was tired and hungry. He was sure his family was upset, and the bump on his head hurt. How good it would be to get home! Maybe he had found that Yaqui village he had been so curious about. Right now he didn't care.

It seemed hours after they had left the Yaqui village that the two boys saw the lights of Manzanita. How welcome those lights looked to Benjie!

Every light in the Brave house was on, and even the yard light was shining. There was a lot of excitement in the village. More cars than usual were around the store and gas station.

As they came near Benjie's home, the boys saw Tony's car near the door, along with others. Could this be because he, Benjie Brave, was missing? Surely everyone couldn't be that worried about him!

Benjie could see through the living room window. Tony was there and Juanito and some other people Benjie didn't know. Benjie ran toward the house, shouting, "I'm here! I'm here and I'm OK!"

Benjie turned to thank Tomasito for bringing him safely home, but the Indian boy had disappeared. The night had simply reached out and swallowed him.

Just then Nosey came dashing out from under the porch, barking excitedly.

"What's going on?" Benjie asked.

But Nosey's only answer was more barking, and Benjie couldn't understand that.

"Well, I'll soon know," Benjie said and opened the door and went inside. "Mother, I'm here!" he called. "I found the Yaqui village and Tomasito brought me home. I'm OK, see?"

Benjie stood before his mother, moving his

arms and legs to show he hadn't been hurt. His mother looked at him quickly, but not as Benjie had expected her to.

"That's good, Benjie," she said. "So much has happened I couldn't worry about you, too."

"What?" Benjie asked, afraid for a minute something had happened to Dr. Brave.

"Didn't anyone tell you? There was an awful explosion at the cement plant. Some men were badly hurt. I must go to the hospital. They need all the help they can get. I'm ready, Tony."

Benjie got a quick kiss and then his mother left with Tony Garcia, who was taking her to the hospital.

Benjie looked around the room full of people —women with small children, older school children, and a few men waited. They all looked very serious as they waited for news that they feared would be bad. The telephone at the Brave house was the only one except for the store phone. It was better to wait here because the news would come direct from the hospital. Mrs. Brave would call.

Benjie's glance rested on Juanito, and his

eyes asked the question he couldn't put in words.

"My father is one of those hurt very much," Juanito said. "My mother says to wait. She is at the hospital now."

"Maybe my mother will call with good news," Benjie said. "Come out in the kitchen with me. I'm starved!"

While Benjie ate a sandwich, the two boys listened for the phone. Juanito told how he'd called for Benjie until Tony had come out to get him with news about the explosion.

The boys went in the living room and sat on the floor near the phone. All the other sitting places had been filled long ago. Even the floor was getting crowded. And still the telephone did not ring.

There was mumbling among the men, but none of it in English.

"Are these all Yaqui Indians?" Benjie asked in a low voice.

"Oh, no," Juanito answered. "Not many Yaquis work at the cement plant. They don't like that kind of work."

55

A man who heard what Juanito had said spoke to the boy in an angry voice. Juanito spoke in very fast Spanish. When they stopped talking, Juanito explained to Benjie, "That man is Jose Onato. He is one of the Yaquis who work at the plant, but he wasn't there when the accident happened. He was off on fiesta business. He says the boss fires them when they leave on fiesta work so he thinks he won't have a job now."

Benjie didn't understand all this, but he nodded anyway.

"Jose says he doesn't care. This explosion proves such a thing as this cement plant should not be here."

Just then the phone rang. Nearly everyone jumped as if to answer, but Benjie was the one who did. It was his mother.

"Benjie? Will you please call Roberto Martinez to the phone?"

Roberto came to the phone.

"Roberto," Mrs. Brave said, "these are the names of the men who were not badly hurt. They have been treated and sent home."

As he was told each name, Roberto repeated it to those who waited. The room was very still as he spoke. No one moved or even seemed to breathe.

The people who had waited for the good news left the house quietly. A sigh of patient waiting was soft in the room as those who stayed for more news found better seats.

"Now, may I speak to Juanito Mendoza, please?" Mrs. Brave asked Roberto.

Juanito was worried and awkward. He pulled the phone off the table, making a loud noise.

"It's OK, Juanito," Benjie said. He put the phone back on the table and told his mother what had happened.

"Benjie, please tell Juanito he is to stay with you tonight. Mr. Mendoza is badly hurt and his wife needs to be near him. Juanito would have no one at home. You can help him—we are doing everything we can to make his father more comfortable. I think he will be all right. Now, may I speak to Juanito again?"

Benjie gave the phone back to Juanito. He watched the boy's face as he listened. There was worry and fear there, but he nodded as Mrs. Brave told him he was to stay with Benjie.

"Tell the other people I will phone again soon," she said.

"OK, Senora Brave. Thank you, adios!"

Juanito told the waiting people what Mrs. Brave had said. Worried but quiet, the people settled again into chairs.

As the minutes dragged on into an hour, there was much talk about the cement plant. Some of the talk was in English and, with Juanito to put in a word of explanation now and then, Benjie began to understand some of the problems the people had.

The families all wanted the money from work these big companies like the cement plant hired men to do. Money meant better food and clothes, a nicer house, maybe even a car.

Not everyone agreed. Some people thought that such things as factories were bad for the Indians and Chicanos.

"They spoil our mother earth," one young man said. "The smoke goes up and covers the blue sky. It makes the light of the sun dim."

"Worse than that, these things take our water," said another. "The streams go dry and the water sinks far down into the earth. It is getting harder and harder to get water—all because of the outsiders who break our land into pieces."

Benjie found his eyes getting heavy as the talk went on and on. He wished Charley could be listening. He would understand better, he might even know some answers.

After another hour, the phone rang again. It was Mrs. Brave with the message that all the men had been treated. Only three were seriously hurt. Senor Mendoza was one. The plant foreman was another. And the third was the older brother of the Yaqui boy, Tomasito. Nothing more would be known until the next day.

As Roberto Martinez repeated this, the women began to gather up their sleeping children. The men who had cars offered to take them home or to the hospital.

In a few minutes the house was empty except for a Sioux boy named Benjie Brave and his new Chicano friend, Juanito Mendoza.

Benjie and Juanito both had big brothers away at college. Being together like this now, they seemed almost like brothers themselves.

"Come on," Benjie said to Juanito. "We will put the rollaway bed in my room. I think we can do it, together."

"I do not want to sleep in a bed that is rolling away," Juanito said. "I can sleep on the floor."

"It's not that kind of rollaway bed," Benjie said. "It is a bed that we can fold up and roll away into a closet or something." For once Benjie knew something he could explain to Juanito.

Leading the way, Benjie took Juanito to his room, which tonight he would share with an almost brother.

6 Making Plans

Mrs. Brave did not come home from the hospital until the sun was making the eastern sky pink. Benjie, his eyes still closed, heard her moving around in the kitchen.

Benjie knew what his mother was doing. She would be putting breakfast on the table. Then she would call him before she went to sleep. This was the way it always was when his mother had worked through the night.

Benjie didn't mind getting his own breakfast. He could do that all right. But he did mind eating alone. When Charley and Jean were at home, Benjie liked getting up so that he could eat with them. Now Jean was in high school away from home and Charley was gone, going to some kind of stupid school—that was the way Benjie always thought of it.

Just as Benjie was about to decide he wouldn't get up at all he heard a thump, then a boy's voice, excited and speaking in Spanish.

Hey! Benjie was suddenly wide awake. Juanito was here! He, Benjie, wasn't alone at all. Juanito was in the rollaway bed, where he'd slept last night.

But Juanito wasn't in bed. He was on the floor, all tangled up in the sheets. The foot brace of the bed had folded while Juanito was turning over. The next thing Juanito knew, he was tumbled out of bed, tangled in sheets.

Benjie remembered what a lot of trouble he and Juanito had had with the rollaway bed. They just couldn't get the brace to go in the right place. Finally, tired of the struggle, they had given up.

"The bed won't fall," Benjie had said. "If it does, you won't go far."

And Juanito hadn't gone far, only to the floor. But he wasn't happy about that. And he didn't like it when Benjie laughed. Juanito said things in Spanish which Benjie couldn't understand but gave him the idea Juanito was getting angry.

"I'm sorry, I shouldn't laugh, but it is funny. And you laugh at me sometimes when things happen to me. I'll help you out of this mess."

Mrs. Brave came to see what was going on. She laughed when she saw Benjie trying to get Juanito out of his tangle of sheets. She helped him. Then she showed both boys how to fasten the brace. Each boy took a turn at fixing it in place.

"Tonight you will be all right, Juanito. No problem," she said.

"My father?" Juanito asked, as if afraid to ask, which he was. "Is he—is he. . . ?"

"Your father is doing well, but he was burned badly," Mrs. Brave said quietly. "He will be in the hospital for a long time. Your mother can do a lot to help him get well. She agrees that you should stay here. We will be happy to have you. Benjie will be very glad, I know."

Mrs. Brave smiled at the boys. "Your breakfast is out except for the cereal," she continued. "It's cooking very slowly. Benjie knows what to do. You boys get up now. Eat your breakfast and get ready for school. Make a nice lunch.

You will find all you need in the refrigerator. I'm going to sleep now, but I'll be here when you come home from school."

"We can do a lot of things after school," Benjie said, "maybe even before school." It was going to be wonderful to have someone to do things with and not to be alone.

"You won't have much time this morning before school," his mother answered. "You have things to do, like taking baths."

"Do we have to?" Benjie asked.

"Well, *you* have to. Juanito can do as he pleases. Tony told me what happened to you yesterday. I'm glad you only have a black-and-blue bump to show for your adventure. Juanito, you keep Benjie out of trouble for me."

Juanito just smiled. He knew that was the kind of thing parents sometimes say.

"Goodnight," Mrs. Brave said. "I'll see you when you come home."

"Buenos noches," Juanito answered politely and then looked with a question in his eyes toward Benjie.

"Mom always says goodnight even if it's

morning," Benjie said. "I have to take a bath now. Then we'll eat breakfast."

Juanito followed Benjie to the bathroom. He looked at the big white tub. "I want to take a bath, too," he decided. "OK?"

"Sure," Benjie said. "Here's a towel. You go first. You're company. I'll go out and make our lunches."

Juanito stood by the tub and made no move to turn on the water or take off the pajamas he'd borrowed from Benjie.

"Take a shower if you like," Benjie said. But still Juanito didn't move.

Then it came to Benjie that Juanito's home might not have a bathtub like this. "I'll get you started," he said, and leaned over to turn on the water. "Tell me when it's just right."

"We have a shower in the yard," Juanito said. "We use a bucket of water. We have to haul our water from the well."

The water splashed into the tub and both boys began to laugh. Juanito because this was something different and fun, and Benjie because here was someone who wanted to take a bath.

66

Juanito got into the tub and sat down with a big splash.

"Hey, don't do that!" Benjie yelled. "We'll have water all over the floor."

Benjie finished getting breakfast and made the lunches. Then he went to get his bath.

Juanito was still in the tub!

"Come on, hurry up!" Benjie scolded and laughed at the same time. "We'll be late for school."

While Juanito slapped the towel over his body to dry off he told Benjie why there would be no bathtub in his house, anyway not for a long time.

"A bathtub takes too much water. I see the way it is. We have to go two miles for our water."

"Is it like that for everybody around here?"

"Not everybody," Juanito replied. "Some people live near the well. They can get water easy."

"You should have a gas engine to pump water for you," Benjie suggested. "That's what this house has."

"No money for that," Juanito answered.

As Benjie dressed, he thought about many things. Juanito knew how to take care of himself in the desert, and maybe he even knew about gold mines. But Benjie knew about things like telephones, rollaway beds, and pumps to get water for bathrooms and kitchens. So who was the smarter, or did it matter?

Benjie looked at the clock. Half an hour to eat and get to school! This called for fast work. The boys just made it. The teacher was opening her attendance book as the boys slid into their seats.

At lunchtime, Benjie said, "I don't see Tomasito here. I wish I knew how his brother is. We should have asked Mom."

Juanito nodded, and Benjie went on, "I bet Tomasito did not know about the cement plant explosion until he got home after bringing me to Manzanita. . . ."

"Yaquis stick together," Juanito said. "They will pray for Tomasito's brother. He will get well."

"My dad will do his best," Benjie added. In times like this, Dr. Brave stayed right at the hospital. Benjie was used to that.

And as the days went by, Juan Mendoza and Tomasito's brother slowly grew better. But Juanito's mother spent long hours at the hospital. When Mrs. Brave explained how much Benjie enjoyed having Juanito, she smiled gratefully. It was good to know her son was safe and being looked after.

"Your boy is teaching my boy Spanish," Mrs. Brave added. "You should hear those two! Half the time I can't understand what Benjie is saying."

Mrs. Mendoza did not quite understand this long English speech, but she felt Juanito was being a good boy, and she was proud of him. She would tell his father.

It was certainly true that Benjie was picking up a lot of Spanish. When October came, he heard some of the Indian boys say they weren't coming to school on Columbus Day. Why should they celebrate the day the white man found their beautiful country?

Benjie and Juanito decided that they, too, would stay away from school. Maybe they would do a little exploring of their own. Maybe go to the hills to hunt for piñon nuts. Benjie would have liked to visit the Yaqui village in the daytime, but he knew better by now than to ask to do that. But what about an old mine? He was almost sure Juanito knew of one. *That* would really be exciting.

The boys kept their plans a secret. They had a strong feeling that if they told, there would be no exploring on a school day.

7 Three Explorers

Benjie and Juanito started for school as usual on the morning of Columbus Day. Each boy had his lunch, and Nosey followed Benjie. The old dog was used to going to school and then returning home when Benjie went inside.

As soon as the boys were out of sight of Benjie's house, they dashed into the mesquite brush on the road leading past the hospital. Nosey chased after them.

"Well, I guess we'll be stuck with him all day," Benjie said, sighing.

"It is OK," Juanito answered.

The boys walked for a long time, up and on toward the low hills. The sun climbed up and up. It was fun to look all about and to talk about what this country was like before Columbus and all the other white men who followed had seen it.

"Plenty to eat then, I think," Juanito said. "Deer running around. Fish in all the streams. Almost no deer now, and the streams are dried up."

"All the time?" Benjie asked, thinking of the dry riverbed where he had been lost.

"Si, all the time. Papa says the dams hold the water back. It does not run into the streams."

"But dams are good," Benjie insisted. "Dams help stop the floods. If there weren't dams, there wouldn't be water for fields and gardens. That's what my father says."

"Maybe good, maybe bad," Juanito said, looking ahead. "Look! See the pines. We will find piñon nuts there."

The boys broke into a run, Nosey at their heels. As they got close to the trees, they saw others were ahead of them. Yaqui children were

72

hunting for nuts among the fallen pine cones. One boy was taller than the others.

"Hey," Benjie said. "Somebody else isn't in school on Columbus Day. There's Tomasito."

The Yaqui boy was more friendly out here than he was at school. Benjie asked about his brother who had been hurt at the cement plant. Like Juanito's father, he was getting well, but slowly.

Hunting for nuts was all right, but it wasn't really very exciting. After a while, Benjie said, "Let's go exploring somewhere. We should discover something today."

Juanito's eyes suddenly sparkled with excitement. "OK. I know about an old mine tunnel near this hill. Let's explore it."

"Let's go!" Benjie exclaimed. Then he waited while in Spanish Juanito asked Tomasito to come, too.

Without saying yes or not, Tomasito followed the two explorers.

"Suppose we really find gold," Benjie said. "That would be great."

"Maybe gold, maybe no gold," Juanito said. "But it will be fun."

Following Juanito, the boys made their way along the hillside. They went around rocks, up a way, and down farther. All at once Juanito pointed and said, "Here it is."

All Benjie could see was a black hole in the side of the hill. Big rocks were all around, with mesquite and cactus nearby.

Near the hole leading into the mine were broken rocks that had fallen not too long ago from the roof of the tunnel. If the boys had noticed them, it would have been good. But they were too busy looking for adventure.

"Let's go in," Benjie exclaimed, and started to move ahead of Juanito. Someone grabbed his shirt. It was Tomasito.

"No! Juanito go. Not you. You stay."

Benjie jerked away. "I won't stay out. I'm going in, too. Just as far as Juanito goes, maybe farther. *You* can stay out."

Juanito had already stepped into the tunnel. "Wait for me!" Benjie called. His voice, loud and strong, came back with a strange hollow sound.

"Dark in here," Juanito called back. He

74

waited until Benjie caught up, but Tomasito did not follow.

"Coming?" Benjie shouted back at Tomasito. There was no answer except for a few little rocks falling. Benjie picked one up and put it in his pocket. He could put it in his rock collection at home.

Both boys went slowly, feeling their way with feet and hands. They began to smell dampness. Then Juanito's foot hit water. Slosh!

"Turn back!" Juanito cried. "A big hole here, I think."

Juanito's voice sounded scared. It frightened Benjie. If Juanito, who knew about old mines, was scared, then they should get out. *Now.*

Benjie got to the mine entrance just as small rocks from overhead began to fall. There was a crash behind him as a timber fell. Dust whirled up.

Looking back, Benjie cried loudly, "Juanito! Juanito!"

There was no answer. Juanito was caught in the mine! Benjie had just had time to escape.

"Tomasito!" Benjie yelled at the Indian boy,

who had run a short way down the hillside. "Help! Juanito is in the mine. It's fallen in on him."

Tomasito came running. As the dust settled, the boys looked but could not see Juanito.

Tomasito put a hand to his ear as if to say "Listen."

"Benjie, Tomasito! Help! I'm caught!" came Juanito's voice. "Help!"

"Don't move, we're coming," Benjie called, trying to sound strong and brave.

Very carefully the boys moved toward the place where the old mine entrance had been. They tried not to trip.

"Are you all right?" Benjie called. If Juanito was safe, it was a miracle.

Tomasito darted to one side. There under a fallen timber, with a lot of dirt and small rocks around him, lay Juanito. The log had certainly saved him, but it was wedged so that he could not drag himself out from under it.

Benjie began to pull rocks away, trying to free his friend. He tugged at the timber. It did not budge. Instead, more dirt began to fall.

76

Tomasito grabbed Benjie. He said something Benjie couldn't understand.

"Let go of me," Benjie shouted. "I'm going to get Juanito out. Let go and help me."

Then to Benjie's surprise and anger, Tomasito turned and ran down the hill.

"Is he running away and leaving us?" Benjie asked in alarm.

"He's going for help," Juanito said. "You cannot get me out. The log is too big. Yaquis are fast runners. Tomasito will soon bring help. I am all right for now."

"Sure?" Benjie asked. He sat down beside Juanito. He was ashamed he had not asked Tomasito first what they should do. "Do you hurt any place?"

"No, but this dirt is heavy on my legs."

Nosey smelled around, maybe trying to find a place to dig.

Benjie stopped him. "None of that, Nosey. Juanito doesn't need any more dirt on him."

Nosey sat quietly beside Benjie.

"Juanito, I guess we should have gone to school."

"Si, I think so, too," Juanito said, his voice sounding less certain now.

"My mother will be angry."

"Si, I think so, maybe."

The boys were silent, each thinking. It was late afternoon, and they should be getting home from school. But today they weren't.

Benjie was sure Tomasito was a fast runner, just as Juanito said. He'd go to Tony Garcia's first for help. He'd try to get Dr. Brave, too. After all, Benjie's father was helping Tomasito's brother get well after the accident at the cement plant.

As Benjie thought about this, he wished he knew more about Tomasito and his people. He had only seen his village once, and that was at night. When Charley comes home, he told himself, maybe we can visit Tomasito and Grandpa Jim.

For some reason, plans about doing a lot of things with Charley didn't seem so important now. Juanito, his new friend, his almost brother, kept Benjie from missing his real brother so much.

Benjie looked at Juanito. He was lying still, not moving more than he had to. Not even talking. Benjie got up to see if he could do anything to make his friend feel better. Maybe he could fold his shirt and put it under Juanito's head.

As Benjie looked around, he saw something interesting. It had marks on it, almost like writing. It looked like a piece of an old flowerpot. Benjie picked it up and put it in his pocket. Another stone to add to his rock collection.

"Are they coming?" Juanito asked. "Please look."

Benjie stepped out where he could see the valley road better. No car coming.

"Not yet, Juanito. Help will come soon."

"Tony is not home maybe," Juanito said, sounding tired.

"Then Tomasito will find someone else. I know he will."

More waiting. It seemed hours, but really it had been only an hour or so since Tomasito had started for help.

Nosey began to bark. A car was coming at

last. Benjie ran to see if it really was Tony, and it was.

Tony stopped as near the old mine as he could. He got out and so did several men with shovels, ropes, and pickaxes.

Dr. Brave was coming, too. Benjie saw his father's car coming farther down the road.

Everyone scrambled up the hillside, Tomasito leading the way.

"Well, well, my amigos, what are you doing here?" Tony asked.

"Exploring. . . ." Benjie answered. Somehow the whole thing didn't look like a very good idea right now.

The men did not stop to talk. They began to work to free Juanito.

Benjie and Tomasito watched. Benjie wanted to thank the Indian boy for getting help, but this wasn't the time.

"Do not worry," Tony said. "We will get you out, Juanito."

When Dr. Brave and Mrs. Brave got to the mine, the men were lifting Juanito to his feet. He could stand, but he looked pale.

"Gracias," he said, "gracias, Tomasito."

The doctor examined the Chicano boy quickly and then said, "Carry him to my car. I will take him to the hospital. I don't think he is hurt, but we will soon find out. This has been a shock to him anyway. Come, Benjie. You have some explaining to do."

"Si," Tony Garcia exclaimed. "These boys want to discover things like Columbus did. They just found a lot of trouble."

Benjie looked around for Tomasito. He had disappeared. Going to his village, Benjie thought. He won't let us help him.

As Dr. Brave drove toward the hospital, Juanito and Benjie told their story. Nosey whined a little.

"And all because you wanted to get even with Columbus because he discovered America," Dr. Brave said and laughed. He didn't scold. He seemed to think it was funny.

"Will Juanito be OK?" Benjie asked, not feeling at all like any explorer.

"I think he's fine," Dr. Brave answered. "I'll bring him back to our house tomorrow. We'll put him in the ward with his father tonight. Juan Mendoza will get a kick out of his boy's adventure story."

Then Mrs. Brave spoke in her best I-mean-it voice. "As for you, young man, you are having a hot bath and going right to bed."

"Yes, Mother," Benjie answered.

There didn't seem to be anything else to say.

8 Fiesta's Coming!

It took some talking, but Benjie got his mother to agree.

As they drove to the hospital, she said, "If it's all right with Mrs. Mendoza, Juanito can spend the rest of the week with us. But no more skipping school and no exploring."

"Si," Benjie answered and grinned.

Juanito walked a bit stiffly because he was sore from bruises. But he had no broken bones.

"You are a lucky boy," Dr. Brave told him.

Mrs. Brave spoke to Mr. and Mrs. Mendoza, and they gladly let Juanito go home with Benjie.

Juanito had some special news. Benjie could feel it. "Tell me what's happened," he begged.

"It's the fiesta," Juanito began. "My family is thankful I am all right. They will give food to help the Yaquis make a good fiesta. That's what we do to say thank you."

"But is this fiesta time?" Mrs. Brave asked. "All Souls Day is in November. Isn't that the next fiesta?"

Juanito shook his head, "Yaquis can have a fiesta anytime. This is a fiesta of promise."

"Wait!" Benjie said. "Let me guess. Is it because Tomasito's brother and the other men hurt at the cement plant are getting well?"

Juanito nodded. "And my father is getting well, too, and I wasn't hurt."

Mrs. Brave said, "I remember Tomasito's brother. Something heavy fell on his foot. We were afraid at first he would always have trouble walking. But his foot is healing now. He will be fine. It's really a miracle he's all right."

"What is that word you say," Juanito asked, "when something very good happens, a thing you can't explain?"

"Miracle? Is that the word?" Mrs. Brave asked. "Maybe you say milagro."

"Milagro—that's it!" Juanito exclaimed. "Tomasito and his family made a promise to the Blessed Virgin of Guadalupe. They promised to honor the Blessed Virgin with a fiesta if Manuel gets well. Milagro! So now his family gives a fiesta of promise, a *manda pahko*. My family will give food because we are thankful my father is getting well."

"I see," Mrs. Brave said.

Benjie asked, "Is it just Tomasito's family giving the fiesta?"

Juanito shook his head. "Everybody gives the fiesta," he said, spreading out his arms as if to take in all the Yaquis.

"Let's go see what they are doing," Benjie said eagerly. 'Maybe we can help."

"No, no!" Juanito said quickly. "We do not go unless they ask us. My family sends food. We do not go now. But when the fiesta is ready, somebody will ask us to share the 'flower.' But we will wait."

"Wait, wait!" Benjie said. "You know I just

went to Tomasito's village once. And that was an accident. I get tired of waiting."

"You'll be in school. Remember?" Mrs. Brave said. She looked straight at Benjie and then at Juanito.

"Yes, Mother," Benjie said.

"Si, senora," Juanito said in a voice like a small echo.

At the end of the week, Tony Garcia came to get Juanito to take him to the Mendozas.

Benjie looked sad. Having Juanito visit was almost like having a brother his own age. He still missed Charley, although not as much as at first.

But Juanito said, "You come to see me sometime. My mama will make tacos, enchiladas, and frijoles."

Thinking about that cheered Benjie. And school was better now. He had made other friends. But the Yaqui boys still paid little attention to him, although Tomasito sometimes smiled a greeting.

Benjie wished he could see Tomasito more often, but the boy did not come to school every day. Tomasito had to work whenever he could because his family needed the money he earned.

Benjie heard some of the boys talking about the Yaqui fiesta and Tomasito's special part. He was in the matachini group—but who or what that was was a mystery to Benjie.

When Benjie asked Juanito, "What is a matachini?" Juanito raised his eyebrows in a way that meant this was something hard to explain.

"A matachini is very important in a fiesta," he said. "He does a lot of things. Maybe dance, maybe play the guitar or violin. I do not know what Tomasito does. Anyway, he helps Grandpa Jim get things ready."

On Friday, Juanito and Benjie worked for Tony Garcia and then went riding. This time Benjie rode Marco Polo and Juanito rode the donkey.

Benjie rode ahead of his friend. Off in the distance was the Yaqui village. Benjie guided the pony in that direction. Pretty soon he could see the wooden crosses in the yards. He could even see the little adobe church with its open front. There were bright things around the church—

later, Benjie found out they were ribbons and cloth and paper flowers.

The Yaquis think the flower is the good heart of the earth, Benjie learned. If you feel happy inside about a person, you share a flower. You want good thoughts and you have lots of flowers if you believe as the Yaquis do.

Benjie stared toward the village. "Suppose I just ride right over there?" he said to himself. "It won't hurt."

Then Benjie pulled back on his pony's bridle. No! Juanito had told him not to go until he was asked. Once this had made Benjie angry. Now he understood a little better that the Yaquis liked to invite their guests in their own way. So, it was wait again, but Benjie could do it.

He couldn't help feeling curious about all that was going on. At the store in Manzanita on Saturday he saw boxes of canned food, bags of corn-meal, bottled drinks, and sacks of beans carried from the store to Yaqui cars.

Benjie got what his mother had sent him for. He walked home with Nosey following. How long would it be until the fiesta, the *manda pahko*, Benjie wondered. And would he really be invited?

In the house, Benjie put the milk in the refrigerator and the coffee on the shelf. There was no one at home. Both Dr. and Mrs. Brave were at the hospital. Now, Benjie thought, if only Charley or Juanito were here. . . .

Just then the telephone rang.

The voice Benjie heard over the telephone made him gasp. It was Charley!

"Hi, kid!" Charley said. "Get ready for a surprise."

Benjie was so excited he could hardly answer. Hadn't he just been wishing and thinking about Charley?

"Hi, Charley, where are you?" he asked.

"I'm in Tucson, but I'm coming home this Thursday on the late afternoon bus. I hope you can all meet me at the bus stop. OK?"

"Sure. Mom and Dad are at the hospital. I'll tell them. Are—are you quitting school?"

"Of course not. This is just something special. I'll tell you when I see you. Everything's OK."

When Charley said good-bye, Benjie put the phone down and thought how good it would be to see his big brother.

Benjie called the hospital to tell his mother and father the news. Only his mother was worried. Why was Charley coming home now she wondered. Thanksgiving was a month away. She was afraid something was wrong.

All Benjie could say was, "He'll tell us when he comes."

The rest of the afternoon Benjie spent working in his room, getting his new treasures out so Charley could see them.

The old softball had the place of honor. Around it Benjie placed some funny little bowls he had made from the leathery linings he'd found inside a giant cactus. Tony Garcia had shown him how to find them.

Benjie had rocks of different kinds. A boy can't live on a desert and not collect rocks. The two best pieces were those he had found near the mine tunnel.

Benjie turned one over in his hand. He had taken it out of his pocket that night after Juanito was in the hospital. It still looked to Benjie as if there were marks like writing on the rock. And when he washed the other rock he'd picked up then, he saw it had a pretty green streak. Would Charley like his rock collection or just smile?

The next day after church, Dr. Brave said, "I want to drive over near the Yaqui village. I have something I promised to give a woman for her baby."

"May I ask Juanito to go with us?" Benjie asked. The boys had sat together during church, and Mrs. Mendoza had not yet started home.

"Of course. Juanito knows more about what is going on in the village than I do."

On the way, Juanito told a little more about the fiesta. "It is not as big as Easter—but it's fine. Tourists will not come to a fiesta of promise as much. It is for the people themselves."

When they got near the village, they saw a very busy place. Dr. Brave stopped the car at a house some distance away. The mother he wanted to see came out.

Benjie looked toward the Yaqui village. Girls and women were making paper flowers. Some were sweeping the churchyard and cleaning. Women were cleaning fire pits, getting them ready for big cooking pots. Everyone, Benjie thought, looked happy.

"There's Grandpa Jim and Tomasito and some of the other big kids!" Benjie said with excitement.

Dr. Brave was ready to leave. "I have to get back to the hospital, so I'll just turn around here and drop you boys at home," he said.

Dr. Brave drove a little closer to the village to turn the car and a man waved to him. It was one of the Yaqui leaders. He came over to the car.

"He is a maestro," Juanito said in a low voice. "Very important."

"Hola, amigo!" the maestro said to Dr. Brave. "It is good to see our doctor here. We are happy. We want to share much 'flower.' Saturday is the fiesta of promise for Manuel and the others."

"For my father, too," Juanito said.

The maestro smiled. "It will be a fine fiesta. We all have 'good heart' to share."

"And we have 'good heart,' too," Dr. Brave answered. "Please take this. It is for the limosna," and he handed a fiesta offering to the maestro.

"Thank you, Dr. Brave. We will all share 'flower' together," the Yaqui man said, taking the money.

94

All the way home, Benjie thought about the fiesta.

"They are bringing a deer dancer from Mexico," Juanito said.

"A deer dancer?"

"Si. Long, long ago the Yaqui people made dances when they went to hunt the deer. They wore rattles and tied deer heads to their own heads. Colored ribbons were on the deer heads. That's the deer dance. It is very hard, people say. A boy needs a long time to do it well. No one here can do it. So deer dancers come from Mexico."

"I've got to see that!" Benjie exclaimed.

Before going to sleep that night, Benjie went over what he had learned about the Yaqui people. Then he thought about Charley coming on Thursday. He could hardly wait.

Would Charley know about the Yaquis? Or would this be something he, Benjie, could tell Charley?

9 News to Share

Benjie thought Thursday would never come. But it did, and even the school day finally ended.

When school was out, Benjie didn't stop to play with Juanito. He ran home as fast as he could go.

The good rich smell of meat roasting and sweetness of chocolate cake met Benjie as he opened the door.

"Hi, Mom—it sure smells good here!"

"We'll have what Charley likes best for dinner," Mrs. Brave said. "Here's a glass of milk and a small cake just for you. After you've eaten, clean up a little and then we'll go to the bus stop. After we meet Charley, we'll drive to the hospital and get your father."

Benjie sat down to eat his cake and drink his milk. He thought about Charley coming. It had been nearly two months since he had seen him. Would his big brother look the same? Would he really be the same?

When the last bite was gone, Benjie said, "Thanks, Mom, that was the best snack ever."

His mother laughed. "At least the best for two days. Remember that warm gingerbread on Monday? Now go on and get cleaned up. Put on a better shirt. That one looks pretty bad."

Benjie went to his room, pulling off his old shirt as he went. When he had finished cleaning up, he looked at his treasures. He had already put them out for Charley to see. That rock with the green streak—he had never seen one just like it. But he was almost sure it wasn't gold. Maybe Charley would know.

When the bus stopped at Manzanita, Charley was the only one to get off. He carried his small suitcase. This didn't look as if he had come home for very long. Benjie felt a small twinge of disappointment.

"How goes it, kid?" Charley asked, roughing Benjie's hair as he always did.

Benjie grinned, while Nosey jumped from one to the other, barking as hard as he could.

Charley kissed his mother and said, "You look great. How's Dad?"

"Just fine. Busier than ever. We'll drive to the hospital and get him now."

On the way to the hospital, the three Braves caught up on news of each other. Mrs. Brave told about letters from Jean. But neither Benjie nor his mother asked the question they most wanted answered. Why had Charley come home when it wasn't vacation time? He wasn't sick. That was plain to see.

While the family was eating chocolate cake, Charley answered their unspoken question.

"I know you're wondering why I came home during the week like this," he said.

"You're right," Dr. Brave said, "so let's have it, good or bad."

"I think it's good," Charley said. "Only I won't be home for Thanksgiving. That's why I came now."

"Not coming for Thanksgiving!" Mrs. Brave exclaimed. "I don't understand."

"Let me begin over," Charley said. "You know I want to be a lawyer and help our people with some of their old land claims."

"But you won't be a lawyer for a long time," Dr. Brave reminded him.

"I know. But a group of Indians have gotten together on some of their land problems. They sent a committee to the college to see Indian law students. Three of us were chosen to meet with them during Thanksgiving vacation. I was one of those chosen. I don't really think I know enough to help them much yet. But I want to learn from them just what they think the problems are. We will talk about some of the old treaties. We'll look into new land laws. We'll try to find out what we can do and what we can't do."

"That sounds good," Mrs. Brave said.

"So that's why I came home now," Charley

added. "I didn't want to wait until Christmas. I'll miss seeing Jean at Thanksgiving, though."

"I'm proud of you, Charley," Dr. Brave said. "We told you we are behind you in what you want to do. And we are."

"Of course, Charley," his mother added. "It's all right."

Only Benjie had nothing to say. He didn't understand why it was so important to Charley to help Indians he didn't even know. But whatever Charley wanted to do, Benjie would try to understand. Anyway, Charley was here now, and Benjie could understand that.

Suddenly Charley spoke directly to his brother. "How about a day with you tomorrow? We'll go anywhere you want to go. Play ball, anything. How about it?"

"Really? Just us two?" Benjie felt happy all over.

"It's a school day," his mother began, but his father interrupted.

"I don't think there will be much school until after the fiesta. That's all I hear at the hospital. The Yaquis are doing this or that, the deer dancer is coming, there will be new matachinis, and so on."

"What fiesta is this?" Charley asked. "Pascua fiesta at Easter is the big thing in Tucson, but that's a long time away. Maybe you can come for that."

"Maybe," Dr. Brave said. "Right now we're learning about a fiesta of promise. One of the Yaqui families is giving the fiesta. *Manda pahko* they call it. It's a thank-you to the Blessed Virgin for healing Tomasito's brother and two other Yaqui men who were hurt in the explosion."

Benjie added, "Juanito's father was hurt, too. Now he is almost well. The Mendozas are giving an offering for the fiesta. It's the Yaquis' fiesta, but I guess just about everyone in Manzanita goes. Now we can all go together."

"I'm glad I'm here to see it with you," Charley said.

Just as he spoke there was a knock at the door. Benjie ran to open it.

There stood three little Yaqui girls. One held out a beautiful red paper flower.

Speaking in Spanish, the little girl said slowly, "For the doctor, for senora, for you, and for him," as she looked from Benjie to Charley. "There will be a fiesta on Saturday."

When Benjie took the flower, the little girls turned and ran.

"What does that mean?" Charley asked.

Then Benjie explained what he had learned from Juanito. "When Yaquis tell you there is going to be a fiesta, it is really an invitation to come."

"Yes," Dr. Brave added, "the maestro asked us, or rather told us, about it last Sunday. I feel honored that we are asked to come. The people of this village don't make fiestas to entertain tourists."

"How lucky I am here now," Charley said, and Benjie thought how lucky he was to have his big brother here to share this special time.

The family sat up late, talking about many things. About Jean away at boarding school. About the hospital and how people were coming from far away to get help. About the explosion at the cement plant and the way the people felt

about it. Benjie told about Tony Garcia and riding Marco Polo and Lightning. He talked about Juanito, too.

"Things are looking up a bit for you, I think," his brother remarked.

"I still don't like this place as well as South Dakota. But it's better since Juanito is my friend," Benjie admitted. "He's almost a brother."

"I remember Mother wrote about Juanito staying here for a while," Charley answered.

The minutes ticked away into hours. Mother didn't send Benjie to bed at the usual time. As long as he was getting a vacation from school next day it really didn't matter.

At last, even Benjie knew he must go to bed. His eyes just wouldn't stay open any longer. But first he had to show Charley his treasures.

"Come and see some things I found in the desert and at that old mine," he said as he went toward his room, Charley following him.

There was the old softball in the center of the shelf. Charley smiled when he saw that. All around the ball were things Benjie had found or made since he had come to Manzanita. The little cactus bowls, a box of piñon nuts, some dried manzanita berries, and many rocks.

Charley picked out the rock with the green streak in it. He turned it this way and that.

"Where did you say you found this?" he asked.

Benjie told him about the day the mine tunnel caved in on Juanito. "I found this, too," he said."Look, it has these funny marks on it."

Charley looked at what Benjie was holding out to him.

"This isn't a rock, Benjie. It's a shard, a piece of very old pottery. People who know about shards can find out a lot about who lived in a place hundreds of years ago, maybe thousands of years."

Charley went on to tell that maybe this shard could tell about Indians who had once lived here, Indians who might have come from far away, perhaps even from South America.

"Where did you find out all this stuff?" Benjie asked. He was more interested than he wanted to show.

"I learned this from some books in the library at that college I'm going to—that college you think is stupid," Charley said in a teasing way. "But tomorrow you can show me where you found these things. You know where to go, and I don't. I think that old mining tunnel has some secrets in it. Maybe we can learn one or two of them."

Benjie went to bed with his head full of puzzling thoughts. As he tried to think his way through them he came back to one word, school. It was in a school called college that Charley had found ways to unlock secrets. Tomorrow Charley, Benjie's big brother, would help him learn some of the old mine's secrets.

But Juanito, Benjie's almost brother, knew the secrets of the desert. He knew how to live with the desert now, not a thousand years ago.

10 Adventure with Charley

Benjie didn't have to be called twice the next morning. The minute he heard Charley moving about, he was wide awake.

There were a few delays such as dressing, eating breakfast, and making a lunch before Benjie's day with Charley could really begin. But at last they were ready to leave.

"Have fun, boys," their mother said. "I'll expect you home in time for dinner."

"We'll manage that," Charley answered. With Nosey at their heels, the boys started out.

The dog didn't stay close to them all the time. He often darted out to chase a jack rabbit or bark at a bird or animal along the way.

Charley stopped and breathed deeply. "This desert air is great," he said. "It's so clean, and it has a different kind of smell. I noticed it when we first came here. After living in a city for a while I notice it more than ever."

Benjie hadn't thought much about the desert air. It was what you breathed because it was there, all around. There wasn't any choice. Now he noticed what Charley was talking about. It did smell good.

"You know," Charley continued, "the Indians were close to all this. The sun, the moon, the earth. They didn't fight nature. They lived with earth mother."

"I guess you're right," Benjie said. "That night when the explosion came, some of the people said things like that. One of them said something about earth mother, but I don't exactly remember."

The boys walked along silently for a time. Benjie had trouble keeping up with Charley's long steps, so Charley walked more slowly.

Two buzzards circled over a low rocky hill.

They flew around and around and settled. The boys could no longer see them.

"Let's go see what they found," Benjie said.

"OK," Charley agreed, and they walked on to the foot of the rocky hill. They began to climb up. The buzzards with a hoarse cry of anger flew away. The big birds found a resting place on a nearby hill.

When the boys reached the place where the buzzards had been, they found a dead jack rabbit. An empty shotgun shell was near it.

Charley picked up the shell. "Hunters," he said. "No one should hunt out here. Wild animals have enough trouble with each other. They don't need men with guns coming, too. Not here on the desert."

"Juanito says rabbits are good to eat. His family hunts them. Maybe the Yaquis do, too."

"This rabbit didn't feed anybody," Charley said.

"It's feeding the buzzards."

"You're right," Charley agreed. "And buzzards need to eat, too, don't they?"

The boys hiked on. Benjie pointed out where

the piñon pines grew. Then far ahead he saw the hillside where the old mine was.

Charley walked around the entrance to the mine. He could see it was too dangerous to try to go into the tunnel. He found an old tree branch and Benjie found a smaller one. The boys prodded the earth, poked at it, and scraped away crusted dirt when they could.

Every now and then Charley found a rock or a piece of what Benjie still thought looked like a broken flowerpot. Benjie found a few pieces to add to the growing pile of treasures.

The purple haze of early morning was gone. The sun was high now. Its light made the red mesas look bright and made Benjie squint.

Suddenly Charley stopped his work. "I'm hungry, kid. How about getting into this lunch? I can use some water to drink."

Benjie opened the lunch Mrs. Brave had packed. There was a thermos of cold fruit juice.

"Our mom—she's the greatest!" Charley exclaimed.

"I'll say," Benjie agreed. "And you know something else? She's glad I found Juanito, and

110

she says he can stay with me anytime. When he's around, I feel like I have a brother my age, almost."

As they talked, Charley scraped the dirt from one of the rocks. He used an old pocket knife.

Benjie couldn't see anything special about the rock, but Charley kept scraping it. Benjie leaned against a dirt pile and watched.

Then Charley exclaimed, "Look, Benjie. I thought I'd find more rocks like yours, and I have. Here's one even bigger, and look at that wide green streak."

"It'll be pretty when it's clean," Benjie said, but there wasn't any reason to get excited.

"Pretty! Do you know what this green streak means?" Charley's dark eyes sparkled.

"No-o," Benjie admitted.

"It's copper. There's a rich vein of copper here someplace. Men came here to look for gold. They didn't find it, so they left this tunnel. They didn't even bother to close it because they didn't think there was anything of value here. They didn't pay any attention to this copper ore—if they even saw it."

Now Benjie was excited, too.

"Maybe it will be a big copper mine like the Dundee Mine. I've heard about that. Then everybody around here could be rich. They could have cars and better houses and all kinds of good things."

When Benjie stopped for breath, Charley spoke, and his voice was serious.

"I'm afraid it wouldn't work out that way. In the first place, the Dundee Mine is wearing out fast. When a big company can no longer make a lot of money, the company moves out. It finds a new place that looks good and does the same thing again. The company hires a lot of people to work in the mine. That's OK, as long as it lasts. Only people worry more now about what happens to our earth mother while the mine is new and rich. There's a good way to use things, and a stupid way. Wait, I've got an idea."

Charley picked up one of the rocks with copper ore and said, "Listen, Benjie, listen to me with both your ears. We mustn't tell anyone about what we found today."

"Why?" Benjie asked. He thought good news

should be shared, not kept a secret.

Now Charley picked up one of the pottery shards. "I'll take this back to school with me. I'll show some of the copper ore to men who know about that. For now, we'll keep still, except to tell Dad and Mom."

Again Benjie asked why.

"This is Indian land, Benjie, or most of it is. It may not belong to the people who live here now, but someplace there is a paper that will tell me who owns it. I want the Indians to have this mine and all the copper ore in it. But it may take a long time to work things out. So now we forget we know about it. OK?"

Charley put out his hand and as man to man he and Benjie shook hands.

"I'll never tell."

"Good, let's go," Charley said and let Benjie's hand go. "Where's that hound dog? Nosey! Nosey!"

Nosey came running from a lizard chase.

Benjie and Charley put the rocks and pottery pieces in the backpack that had held their lunch. It was time to go home.

11 Into the Wind

The fiesta! Benjie felt as if he'd been waiting all his lifetime for Saturday, and now here it was.

He knew from what Juanito had told him that the fiesta of promise would begin at sunset. The Mendozas would go a little earlier because they were in a way taking part, too. Mr. Mendoza was now out of the hospital, and of course Juanito had escaped being seriously hurt at the mine.

Charley wanted to visit the cement plant and stop at the hospital, but Benjie was not interested. He stayed home and played ball with Juanito and some of the other Chicano boys.

When it was late afternoon, the Brave family left for the Yaqui village.

"You must come in time to see the pascolas open the fiesta," Juanito had warned. "If you are late, you will not see it or hear it."

"Will there be a lot of noise like firecrackers and stuff?" Benjie had asked.

But Juanito's answer didn't help much except to make Benjie all the more curious. "No firecrackers. You will see and hear when the time comes."

Charley drove the car along the rough road until it ended near the village. Then all the Brave family walked to the church and became part of the happy, brightly-dressed crowd.

Many people smiled a welcome and made a place for the doctor and his family to stand with them.

Benjie looked around, trying to see everything at once. There was a lot to see. Tomasito's family had worked hard to make their yard a special place.

There was an altar in the household ramada. It was covered with a white cloth which had colored paper flowers pinned to it. There were candles on the altar, and a rug in front of it. Statues of some of the saints had been placed on the altar.

A feeling of breathless waiting filled the village. Even Benjie, who had never seen such a celebration as this, felt a kind of hushed gladness. Was this the "flower" people spoke of? The "good heart" that Juanito told about?

Benjie wanted to ask a lot of questions, but this didn't seem the time.

Someone came close to Benjie, and a voice whispered, "A fine fiesta, si?" Of course Benjie knew that voice—it was Juanito's.

Before Benjie could answer, music began. Was the tune played on a flute? Benjie couldn't be sure. The music came again, soft, but easy to hear. It was like a bird singing nearby, but hidden.

"Listen," Juanito whispered excitedly. "The pascolas open the fiesta with that song. It is called 'The Canary.'" And he smiled because the song was so beautiful.

Benjie saw Charley smile, too.

116

The song was played several times. Then a flutter of excitement passed through the crowd.

"The deer dancer!" people said softly.

There he was, with the deer singers and pascolas near him. The pascolas were the older men in the fiesta. They were sometimes like clowns and made the children giggle. They moved near the young man as he went to the place which was waiting for him.

The deer dancer wore a headdress made to look like a deer's head. Red flowers and ribbons decorated the horns. A belt of deer hoof rattles was fastened around his waist. He carried gourds that he shook gently as he walked along, each step light and nearly dancing.

Soon the deer dancer began to dance, taking a turn with each of the four pascolas, one after the other.

"He is one fine deer dancer," Benjie heard people around him say. "Tomasito says he comes all the way from Mexico," Juanito reminded Benjie. "It takes years to learn a deer dancer part. He has to have good dreams of it first. No one here has the dreams."

Benjie wanted to ask more about the deer dancer, but there wasn't time. Too much was happening.

The pascolas brought Tomasito's family into a group. Dancing with them, around them, and leading them with dancing steps, they went into the house.

"Will they come out?" Benjie wondered.

A few minutes went by, then out they came, carrying small statues of saints. They put these on the altar with the other saints.

"Why are they doing that?" Benjie whispered to Juanito, who still stood near him.

"Because the holy ones from the house must celebrate, too," Juanito explained. "No holy one must be left out at this happy time."

It was dark now, except for the light from the little fires around the yards. There was a cool breeze, and sometimes people stood near a fire for a few minutes, warming themselves. But no one stayed by a fire for long. Too much was happening.

"The matachinis!" Juanito said, forgetting to keep his voice low.

Benjie looked where Juanito was looking. Sure enough, here came men and boys with bright-colored paper ribbons fluttering from their headdresses.

"There's Tomasito—I can see him!" Benjie exclaimed.

The matachinis carried shovels filled with hot coals. Benjie wanted to know why.

"They stay near the deer dancer and the pascolas to help keep them warm," Juanito explained. Benjie didn't see how this really helped. Anyway the men and dancers were moving about so much there seemed little chance of their being cold.

Tomasito wore a splendid headdress with strips of red crepe paper hanging from it. He carried a wand decorated with colored feathers.

One of the men from Manzanita was standing near Charley. He tried to explain to Charley and his parents what some of the fiesta meant.

"There is much 'flower' here. All these bright feathers and colored ribbons are 'flower.' It is part of the 'flower of the good heart.' Many Yaquis gave things for the fiesta, all kinds of things. It is thanks to the Virgin because a sick one or a hurt one is now well."

Benjie listened to this and nodded as if he understood it all, although he wasn't really sure he did. He was too busy looking and listening to ask questions. He watched every move Tomasito made. Dancing with the matachinis, Tomasito did not seem like the same quiet, sometimes unfriendly boy who came to school just part of the time.

The dancing and music was going on all the time now. The matachinis made a circle around a pole as the singing and drum beating continued. Benjie moved along with the crowd to watch.

Streamers hung from the pole. The matachinis caught the streamers and danced around the pole, weaving the bright-colored strips in and out.

"That's 'flower' too," Juanito said.

"It's like winding a maypole," Mrs. Brave added.

People watched the dancers and laughed at the funny things the pascolas did. But by and by

Benjie's attention wandered from watching. He sniffed. Wonderful, spicy smells filled the air. Suddenly his dinner seemed long ago. When was the food going to be served?

By midnight everyone was as hungry as Benjie. Tomasito's father called the pascolas and the deer dancer to the long outdoor table. They ate stew with big pieces of meat, tortillas, and tostadas, and drank coffee. Benjie's mouth watered.

When the deer dancer and pascolas finished, the matachinis were called to the table. Girls in bright-colored fiesta dresses hurried here and there, taking hot food to the tables, filling coffee cups.

"I'm going to starve!" Benjie whispered to Charley. "How can you stand there and not be hungry?"

"Who says I'm not hungry?" Charley asked. "We'll eat when it's our turn. This is the Yaqui way of doing things."

The guests were served last, with Tomasito and other members of his family standing near. They held candles to light the guest tables. And if Dr. Brave's plate was filled time and again, it was surely a way of saying a thank-you in helping the sick get well.

After everyone—even Benjie—had eaten all he could, the dancing began again.

So much had been happening that it came as a surprise to Benjie. He hadn't seen Grandpa Jim anywhere. "Is anything wrong?" he asked Juanito. "You said Grandpa Jim had a big part in the fiesta."

"Look over there," Juanito said. Then Benjie saw Grandpa Jim, dressed as one of the maestros. He was standing at the altar and seemed to be giving a short speech or prayer. Benjie couldn't tell which. He noticed, however, that the people always listened with respect while Grandpa Jim spoke.

When the deer singers began their chant, the deer dancer again danced with each of the pascolas. This time, Benjie knew better what to expect and laughed with the crowd. Each pascola tried to make the deer dancer laugh or stumble. The deer dancer had his part in the fun. He made faces as if he wanted to laugh but wouldn't give in. He acted as if he were falling, but he always came up on his feet, dancing. No pascola made an awkward clown of that deer dancer.

"He's good!" Juanito laughed and clapped, and Benjie joined in clapping, too.

Finally Dr. Brave said, "I think we should go home. I have to be at the hospital early tomorrow."

"The fiesta ends before the sun is up," Mr. Mendoza said. "The matachinis will unwind the streamers from the pole. There will be speeches."

"I wish I could stay," Dr. Brave said. "Before I go, I must speak to Tomasito's father. Where is he?"

"I'll show you," Juanito offered, and led the way.

Dr. Brave explained why he and his family were leaving. "Thank you for sharing 'flower' with us. It is a wonderful fiesta. I am glad we could come and that my big son, Charley, could be here, too."

Tomasito's father smiled and stood proudly as

he looked from one of Benjie's family to another. He knew the fiesta of promise had indeed gone well.

Driving home, Benjie said, "You know, I think the Yaquis are the people of the 'good heart.'"

"Good food and dancing, too," teased Charley.

On the rest of the way home, Benjie was quiet. It wasn't that he was sleepy. He was thinking about Charley's leaving. It seemed so soon.

Charley noticed his brother's serious face. "Come on," he said. "I'm glad you'll miss me, but you've got a good new friend. I hear you two mixing up Spanish and English. I wish I could learn a new language that fast."

The praise made Benjie feel good. "And you can teach me a lot about the desert," Charley continued. "College isn't the only place to learn things. But I do want to get back and do some checking on the questions we have about the old mine."

"I'll keep the secret," Benjie said eagerly.

Dr. Brave said quietly, "As our people say,

'The words will be thrown into the wind and will not be spoken again until the wind wills it.' "

Charley smiled. "I haven't heard that saying for years and years. It really fits this old mine business."

And so next morning Benjie stood with his mother and Charley at the bus stop. Somehow he didn't feel sad this time. For one thing, Charley, and Jean, too, would be home for Christmas, for two whole weeks. And for another thing, there was Juanito—maybe he'd join Benjie and Charley in exploring.

Now the bus was coming, slowing as it pulled up to the stop.

Charley roughed up Benjie's black hair. "I'll be seeing you, kid. OK?"

"Sure, I'll see you," Benjie answered. This time there wasn't a lump in his throat.

He waved as the bus pulled away, headed for Tucson. Then he turned to his mother. "I want to walk home, may I?" he asked.

"Of course," Mrs. Brave answered. "Don't be too long." She understood things about Benjie he didn't really understand himself.

"Come on, Nosey," Benjie called, and the old dog scrambled out of the car and ran after his master.

Mostly Benjie wanted to walk along by himself, just thinking. Maybe college was OK for Charley. He knew a lot about mines and rocks and broken pieces of pottery called shards.

Benjie knew he wouldn't be lonesome. Manzanita wasn't such a bad place after all. Juanito, his almost brother, was here. There were the Yaqui people with their own ways that were different from anything Benjie had known before.

Best of all, Benjie carried deep inside the secret of the old mine. Charley would help the Indians with it. He would see that his Mexican-American friends were not forgotten. And Benjie felt that when the time came, he'd have a part in the planning and changes that would come to Manzanita.

The red mesas looked beautiful today. Had they always looked this way? He breathed deeply, enjoying the clean sharp air the way he and Charley had together just two days ago.

Suddenly Benjie thought of something he wanted to do. He climbed to the top of a nearby hill. The cholla cactus was all around, reaching out prickly arms to catch him. But he stayed out of reach. He was learning to live with the desert.

When he got to the top of the hill, Benjie looked toward the sun, now almost midway in the sky.

Softly to himself he said, "The secret of the old mine is with Charley and me. I throw the words into the wind and will not speak them again until the wind wills it."

He made a throwing motion into the air, then he turned and went down the rocky hill toward home, Nosey following.